THE YELLOW ONE EYED MONSTER

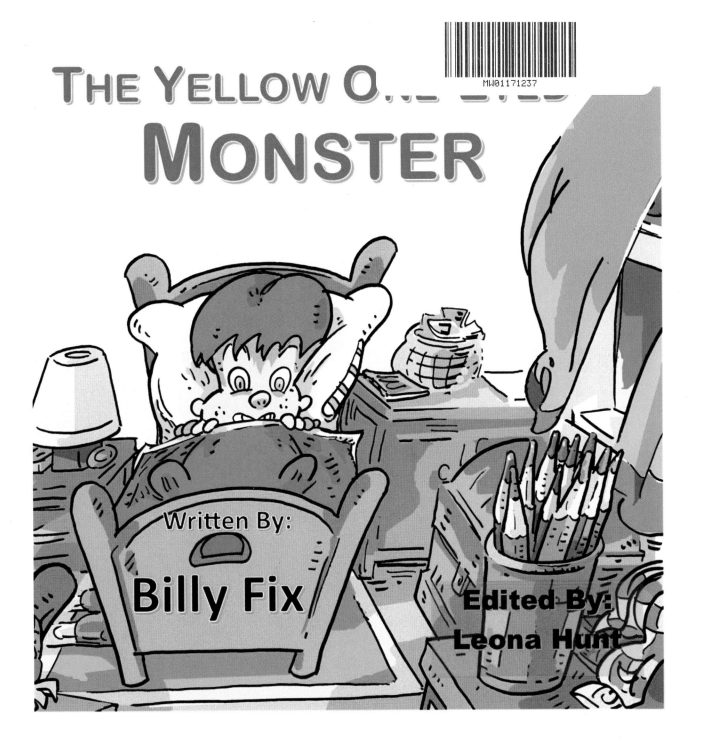

Written By:
Billy Fix

Edited By:
Leona Hunt

The Yellow One-Eyed Monster

Author Bill Fix

Editor Leona Hunt

ISBN: 9798675481477

This Book Belongs to:

_____

A Gift From:

_____

Purchase *The Yellow One-Eyed Monster Coloring Book* at Amazon.com

You Can Purchase the first book in the series, *Daddy Can I Go Fishing?* at Amazon.com

Free Audio Reading of *The Yellow One-Eyed Monster* Go to: https://www.peoplepastor.com

THE YELLOW ONE-EYED MONSTER

By: Billy Fix

I always enjoyed playing with my toys

Neighbors came over little girls and little boys

We played with a ball, and had some great fun

We were very happy, outside in the sun

When dad came home, mom called me in

"Wash your hands," she said, "before supper begins"

My dog, Boxer, and I ran fast as we were able

I sat in my chair. Boxer was under the table.

Fried potatoes, hot dogs, macaroni,

And a big cup of milk.

I watched my sister grab her cup

And crash! It dumped and spilled

Boxer was there and lapped it all up;

Mom took great care and refilled her cup

It was no big deal, but don't act a fool

Mom said, come on, be careful, all of you.

Later, when it was dark outside,

I had enjoyed my fun-filled day

It was very close to bedtime,

So I put my toys away.

I did not like this time of day;

Outside, it was dark

I climbed the steep stairway.

And Boxer, began to bark

I jumped into bed and covered my head

I stayed there till I couldn't breathe

My throat was dry, and I needed a drink

I yelled, "Mom, I need water, please!

I yelled it again, and she finally came

With a glass of water and a kiss

Afraid of the dark, in my room, in my bed,

Not at all, did I like the darkness.

My head under covers, it was hard to breathe

So, I slowly uncovered my head

The air was refreshing, but the room was dark,

I imagined a monster close to my bed

My heart leaped within my chest

When the monster opened his eye.

It was yellow, then it suddenly closed

I was scared, and I shook. Oh my!

Did he see me? Was He Near?

I trembled, with a little boy fear

I would be bold if I had a spear

I'd fight that monster without a tear

I tried to see through the dark.

Where could that monster be?

He opened his yellow eye again

This time, he was close to me.

In my room in the dark,

With the monster close, it seemed;

Should I run for the door?

Or should I cover my head and scream?

Was he a one-eyed monster?

One eye is all I've seen.

He opened it by the window,

He closed it by my door, so I screamed!

33

When the monster shut his eye,

My parents ran up the stairs

They hit the light and the monster?

Had vanished! But where?

I told them the one-eyed monster

Was in my room, and near my bed.

Dad searched around the room.

Look, Billy, there's no monster, he said.

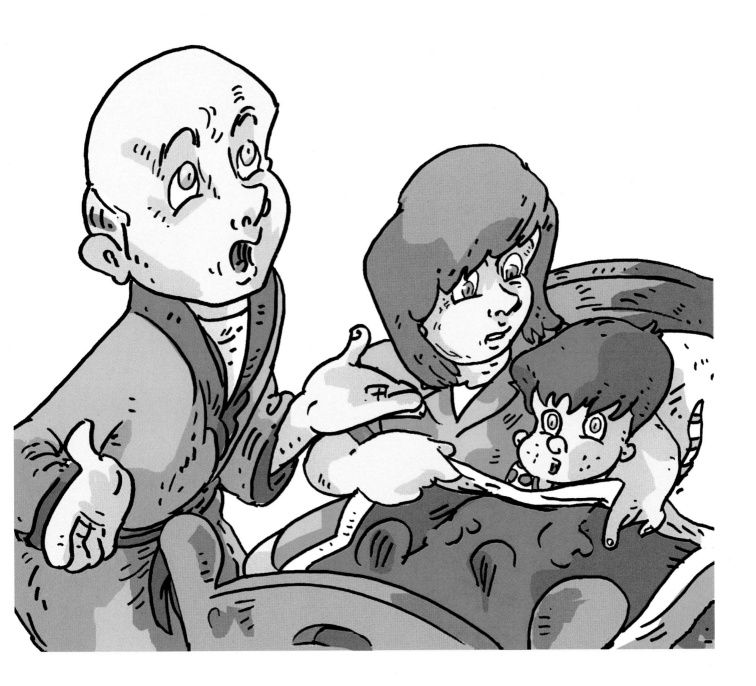

Maybe that monster appeared

Only when it was dark at night.

Mom stood beside me,

While Dad shut off the light.

We patiently and quietly waited.

For the one-eyed monster to show up

Finally, he did. He opened his eye,

I yelled, Dad, make him stop!

Dad turned on the light

And looked where the monster appeared

Mom had seen it, Dad had seen it,

And the yellow one eyed monster, was real!

Dad said, I found the one-eyed monster;

As he motioned in the air

He pointed at a flying bug,

Why should I look? Why should I care?

Amazing! It was a lightning bug,

As it flew within my sight

I watched as it lit up its tail

It shined like a bright yellow eye.

The yellow one-eyed monster

The mystery was finally solved.

It was a flying lightning bug

Only one, had been involved

Dad and mom was there for me.

And Mom said she would stay

With head on my pillow, Mom by my side

I liked falling asleep this way

I fell asleep with mom by my side

I will never forget that night

In my room by my bed; in the dark

Frightened by no monster, but a bug with a light.

Based on a true story from the Author's childhood.

The
End

Made in the USA
Columbia, SC
19 May 2023

16396352R00031